Emerald and the
Friendship Bracelet

Special thanks to Conrad Mason
To Ida Mason

ORCHARD BOOKS

First published in Great Britain in 2023 by Hodder & Stoughton

13 5 7 9 10 8 6 4 2

Text copyright © Working Partners Limited, 2023
Illustrations copyright © Working Partners Limited, 2023
Series created by Working Partners Limited

The moral rights of the author and illustrator have been asserted.

A CIP catalogue record for this book
is available from the British Library.

ISBN 978 1 40836 750 6

Printed and bound in Great Britain by Clays Ltd, Elcograf S.p.A.

The paper and board used in this book are made from wood from responsible sources.

Orchard Books
An imprint of
Hachette Children's Group
Part of Hodder & Stoughton Limited
Carmelite House
50 Victoria Embankment
London EC4Y 0DZ

An Hachette UK Company
www.hachette.co.uk
www.hachettechildrens.co.uk

Daisy Meadows
Author of Rainbow Magic

Emerald and the Friendship Bracelet

Illustrated by
Jo Lindley

Meet the Characters

Alice loves all sorts of arts and crafts. She's great at thinking up clever ways to solve problems, and her inventions are amazing!

Alice

Leo

Leo is always kind and thoughtful. When he's not busy helping his friends or practising his juggling, he loves making things in the craft studio with Alice!

Hopscotch

Hopscotch is one of the Glitterbugs – the Pixies' minibeast helpers. They collect bits and bobs for the Pixies to use, and they look out for anyone having a hard time.

Emerald

Emerald the Jewellery Pixie uses her magical tools to make special trinkets that help fix people's problems.

Grimble & Grumble

The horrible Nixies, Grimble and Grumble, live in a rubbish dump and love casting bad spells to spoil everyone's fun.

Leo's house

Playground

Post Office

Alice's flat

Crystal Bay

Emerald's workshop

The Hive

Cobbletown

Contents

When things are old and start to fray,
Some people just throw them away.
But to us, they aren't quite done:
We see the heart inside each one.

With our friends, the Glitterbugs,
A little magic and some love,
We turn old things into new.
Will you come and help us too?

Love from
The Pixies

Chapter One
Sea Glass

It was a warm afternoon, and the playground of Crystal Bay Primary School rang with laughter as the children spilled from their classrooms.

Stepping into the sunshine, Alice spotted Leo's dad talking to some other parents at the school gate. She smiled and waved. Leo was her best friend, and today she was going to his house for tea.

"Wait for me!" Leo came tumbling out of the classroom behind her, arms laden with his book bag, water bottle and jumper.

"Leo?" A deep voice rang out behind them. Leo and Alice turned to see their teacher holding out three juggling beanbags.

Leo popped them in his book bag. "Thank you, Mr Sandhu. I can't believe I nearly forgot these," he said, grinning. "Show-and-tell day is the *best!*"

Mr Sandhu smiled. "Maybe next time, try not to knock my pen pot over," he said. "But well done on making those beanbags yourself. See you two tomorrow."

Alice grinned at Leo as Mr Sandhu went inside. "I thought your juggling was amazing!" The salty sea breeze blew a strand of brown hair across her face, and she tucked it back into her hairband. She felt in her pocket, checking that the lump of sea glass she had brought to school was still there.

"Ooh, let's see it one more time!" said Leo, dancing up and down with excitement.

Alice giggled. She and Leo both loved to make things, and normally she brought in one of her latest inventions for show-and-tell, like the boat she had made from a milk carton, straws and a balloon.

But today, she had brought something even more special.

The sea glass glowed like a magical jewel as Alice held it up in the sunshine. It was smooth and round, and it fitted perfectly in the palm of her hand. Stripes ran through it in different shades of blue, from a cool turquoise to a deep sapphire. The colours were like the sparkling sea that could be seen from the playground.

"So cool," breathed Leo.

"Best present ever," sighed Alice.

It was Leo who had

found the sea glass, when they went litter-picking last year on the beach near their school. It was washed up on the sand, glimmering in the shallows. Once it had been a chunk of glass, but the waves had worn it into a rounded pebble.

Alice didn't love the sea glass just because it was beautiful. She loved it because Leo had given it to her. They had been friends since they were tiny ... but that was the day they had decided to be *best* friends.

"Best friends for ever," Leo said, echoing Alice's thoughts with a grin.

Then something caught his eye, and he frowned. "Who's that girl?" he asked.

Standing in a corner of the playground was a small, freckly girl with curly red hair. She was clutching her book bag, her big eyes darting all around. She must have been at least two years younger than Alice and Leo.

"That's Ellie," said Alice. "Mum got chatting to her dad in the fudge shop. They've just moved to Crystal Bay, and she's in Year One. I guess her parents haven't come to pick her up yet."

"She doesn't look very happy, does she?" said Leo.

As they watched, a couple of boys Ellie's age ran up to her. Ellie looked startled as they started talking, showing her a Frisbee. *They're asking her to play*, thought Leo. But Ellie just gripped her bag even tighter and shook her head, her cheeks turning pink.

The boys shrugged and ran off,

throwing the Frisbee. But Leo noticed Ellie looking wistfully after them.

"We should go over there," said Leo. But just then, Ellie's dad arrived – a big, fair-haired man in a navy coat. They left together, Ellie huddling close at his side.

"Poor Ellie!" said Alice, shaking her head. "It must be hard starting at a new school when you don't know anyone."

"Especially if you're shy," agreed Leo.

Leo was the least shy person Alice had ever met. He loved performing, whether it was a play, or a song, or a class assembly. Just being with him made Alice feel more confident. *If only Ellie had a friend like I do!* she thought.

"Ready to go, kiddos?" said Leo's dad as they reached the school gates. He wore his usual wide smile and one of his favourite woolly jumpers, knitted by Leo's gran. He was tall, just like Leo, and he had the same springy black curls. "Mum's doing pizza for dinner. Sound good?"

Alice and Leo smiled at each other. "You bet!"

A short while later, the friends darted through the garden doors at Leo's house and across the small grassy lawn. They were heading for a ramshackle wooden shed that stood at the end of the garden, beneath the drooping branches of an old hazel tree.

In the kitchen behind them, Leo's mum was humming to herself and chopping onions and peppers, while Leo's baby brother, Jay, slept peacefully in his pram in the corner. Both of Alice's mums were working today, and they weren't coming to pick her up until later. The friends had an hour until dinner time, which meant an hour of crafting in their studio.

Alice and Leo grinned as they ducked through the door. From the outside, the shed was nothing special. But inside, it was like Aladdin's cave! Every inch of space was crammed with supplies. Colourful wooden shelves were fixed on to the far wall, carefully labelled in Alice's neat handwriting. They groaned under the weight of paint pots, brushes, spools of thread, heaps of cardboard and eggboxes, glue sticks, bags of glitter and lots more besides.

Under a little window was an old wooden desk that Alice's mums had given them, its surface covered in scratches and ink stains. There were two stools tucked under it, painted in a rainbow of colours. Opposite, there were more shelves, loaded with finished projects. There was a rocket ship covered in tin foil, a pottery dinosaur with a long, curving neck, cardboard animal masks made by Leo and a bug hotel made by Alice.

A tatty old Persian rug covered the floor, and from the ceiling dangled a mobile made from dozens of colourful bottle caps which swayed in the breeze from the door.

Alice and Leo had turned the shed into a craft studio together, and it was their favourite place in the world.

"Shall we finish the ladybirds?" asked Leo. He pulled out a stool and sat beside a pair of papier-mâché ladybirds on the desk. "They're dry now. We could paint them!"

Alice smiled. "Actually, I was thinking we could make a picture of the sea glass. I just love all those different blues." She pulled it from her pocket and placed it on the windowsill, where the light fell on it.

"Perfect!" said Leo. "I'll get the paints out."

He had just turned to the shelves at the back of the shed when he saw something flicker through the shed door.

"What's that?" gasped Alice.

They both stared in astonishment. A large butterfly was darting around inside the shed. But it was like no butterfly they had ever seen before. Its wings were changing colour as they watched, shimmering pink, then blue, then gold. Stranger still, wherever it flew,

it left a glittering
trail of golden
sparkles that
drifted and
twinkled in
the air.
"What
IS that?"
breathed Leo.
"It's like
magic!" said Alice.
Suddenly the butterfly swooped
down to the windowsill. And before the
friends knew what was happening, it
was streaking away, carrying something

held tightly in its legs . . .

"My sea glass!" cried Alice.

But it was too late. The butterfly had already disappeared through the open door.

Chapter Two
The Magical Painting

Alice and Leo scrambled out of the shed, hearts racing. They whirled around, looking for the creature. Then Alice pointed. "There it is!"

She had spotted the butterfly hovering over the garden fence, still clutching the sea glass.

"Come back!"

yelled Leo.

They dashed towards the fence, but as they drew close, the butterfly fluttered away again. It flew over the garden gate and along the narrow alley that ran down the side of the house.

"It's gone out into the street," said Alice, clenching her fists with worry.

Leo turned back and cupped his hands round his mouth. "Mum! We're heading out for a minute."

His mum's voice floated back to them from the kitchen. "Come back soon. And don't go far!"

They ran down the alley on to the little terraced street and spotted the glittery golden trail, curving round the corner towards the High Street. The butterfly had already disappeared from view.

"I can't believe it took my sea glass," said Alice. Tears pricked at her eyes. "What if it's just . . . gone?"

"It can't have," said Leo firmly. "We're going to get that sea glass back. Promise!"

They hurried out on to Crystal Bay's busy High Street, dodging tourists and fishermen as they followed the golden trail.

Mrs Briggs from the newsagent waved to them through the window. Mr Kwarteng the postman gave them a wink as he passed by with his niece and nephew. None of them seemed to notice anything unusual about the butterfly flitting by.

"It's heading for the beach," puffed Alice.

They ran past their favourite fish and chip shop, the little post office and the fudge shop, and out on to the quay. The breeze tugged at their clothes, and the smell of the sea filled their nostrils. Seagulls wheeled and cried in the clear blue sky.

Ahead of them stretched the beach, a perfect crescent of bright golden sand. Beyond it, the waves sparkled like a thousand diamonds.

But the butterfly was nowhere to be seen.

Then Leo pointed. "Look!"

There was the glittery trail, curving over the edge of the quay to the beach. The friends hopped down on to the sand. "Huh . . ." said Leo, looking back. "I never noticed that before."

On the wall behind them was an old mural, the paint faded and peeling with age. It was a picture of Crystal Bay. Except, as they peered closer, they realised it didn't look *quite* the same. Some of the buildings were different colours and shapes. Leo's house with its red front door was missing altogether, and so was Alice's modern apartment building on the quayside.

The trail of golden sparkles seemed to stop at the mural.

"Looks like a dead end," said Alice, frowning. "Except . . ."

The friends gasped in amazement.

Something strange was happening to the painting. The colours were changing, becoming brighter and more . . . real. And now the mural was *moving*. The little painted waves lapped at the shore. The clouds drifted through the sky.

"There's that butterfly!" cried Leo, peering closer. "And it's still got your sea glass!"

Sure enough, a little painted butterfly was flitting across the image of the beach. An explosion of tiny pink hearts shimmered around the creature's antennae.

Alice got the most peculiar feeling. "Do you think . . . it wants us to follow?"

"There's only one way to find out." Leo took a deep breath and held out his hand. Alice squeezed it tight.

"Are we really going to . . . step into a painting?"

"A magical painting," said Leo. "At least, I hope it is. Should we give it a try?"

The little butterfly was hovering right in front

of them. It looked like he was *beckoning* them with his antennae now.

"I guess that's the way in," said Alice. "One . . . two . . . three!"

And together, they reached out and touched the spot where the little butterfly was fluttering.

WHOOOOOOSH!

There was a rushing in their ears. Leo yelped, and Alice drew a sharp breath as they were sucked forwards. Their hair and clothes streamed in the wind.

The painting blurred and lights flashed all around them, magical sparkles of colour that twirled and danced like shimmering sequins, until—

WHUMPH.

All of a sudden, they stopped. They were dizzy, but there was solid ground beneath their feet.

"What on earth . . . ?" breathed Leo.

The friends looked around in amazement, hardly believing their eyes.

They really were *inside* the painting.

They stood on the quayside, with the

town laid out in front of them, as real as Crystal Bay. But now, up close, they saw that it wasn't quite the same as the town they had left behind. Alice examined the nearest house. "Hey," she said. "Those bricks aren't real! They're drawn on."

"And the wall is made of cardboard," said Leo. "So is the roof!"

"It looks like . . . a giant shoe box!" Alice gasped. If it had been one of their craft projects, she would have been bursting with pride. Little lolly-stick window frames painted bright yellow were hung with matching curtains.

Tissue paper flowers bloomed from neat hanging baskets by the front door, above a lawn of soft green felt.

They turned to a large pink house covered in white spots. It was a strange shape, and it took them a moment to recognise it.

"It's the biggest welly boot I've ever seen!" cried Leo. "And look – someone's cut out a doorway, right at the heel."

Alice gasped. "Leo, I don't think the boot is big. **I think we've shrunk!**"

Leo spun round, his eyes wide. "You're right," he said. "This is a magical world.

No wonder the painting didn't look the same as Crystal Bay! I vote we explore!"

They set off down a road that looked like the High Street from Crystal Bay. But instead of the fudge shop, there was a candy-striped castle with battlements covered in wrapping paper. And instead of the post office, there was a brightly painted bird box the size of a house, with cotton wool smoke coming out of the chimney.

"Every single building is like one of our craft projects," said Alice in wonder.

A huge grin spread across Leo's face. "This place is amazing!" He leaped and twirled with excitement, and Alice couldn't help giggling.

They wandered down the road, past a driftwood bungalow and a clock tower made from an orange juice carton, until they came out into a square. It was just where the town square was in Crystal Bay, but instead of the familiar bronze statue of a pair of leaping dolphins, there was a building towering over the nearby cottages.

The friends stopped and stared.

The building was shaped like a rainbow-coloured beehive. It glittered and sparkled in the sunlight.

"I wonder how it was made?" said Alice. "Ooh, if only we could go inside and take a look . . ."

Leo smiled. Alice was always trying to figure out how things worked.

"Well, bless my silver earrings, you made it! Welcome, Alice and Leo!"

The friends jumped. Whose voice was that? They spun around and stopped in their tracks.

Scurrying across the square towards them was a little person with a cheerful smile on her face. She had pink skin, big eyes and a pointed nose and ears. Her sparkly green dungarees were decorated with jewels and beads, and her wrists jingled with bracelets as she moved. She was only as tall as the friends' shoulders.

"Who are you?" whispered Alice in amazement. *She looks like some kind of elf...*

"Emerald, at your service!"

said the tiny person. "I'm the Jewellery Pixie!"

Chapter Three
Welcome to Cobbletown

"Nice to meet you," said Leo, sticking

out a hand. Emerald shook it warmly.

Up close, Leo saw that her hair was pale

green and sparkled in the sunlight. It

was held back with a jewelled clip – a

sparkling green gemstone. *An emerald,*

just like her name, thought Leo.

Alice was peering at the work belt that Emerald was wearing. It was hung with a set of golden tools – pliers, a small hammer and a round tool with a lens inside.

"That's my magnifying glass," said Emerald. "It's for making jewellery. And it's magical too!" She clapped her hand to her head. "Oh, twinkling brooches! I almost forgot. Meet my friends!" She stuck her fingers in her mouth and gave a whistle.

A door flew open on the other side of the square, and five more tiny people stepped out of a café made from a broken lunchbox. They grinned and waved when they saw Alice and Leo.

"Ooh! Is it really them?"

"Hello, Alice! Hello, Leo!"

"We're the Pixies!"

"Welcome to Cobbletown!"

The Pixies each wore a sparkly outfit and pointy-toed shoes, and their skin and hair were all different colours.

"We've been waiting for you," Emerald explained.

"It's lovely to be here," said Alice, smiling and waving back. "But—"

"But why?" Leo interrupted.

"Because you two understand the magic of making things," said Emerald with a warm smile. "You have crafting hearts."

Alice's fingers were tingling, just as they did when she was excited about starting a new craft project. "We do," she agreed. "So what is Cobbletown?"

Emerald flung out her arms. "It's a magical world, of course!"

"I knew it," Leo breathed. "And we *have* shrunk, haven't we?"

Emerald nodded.

"Will we stay shrunk for ever?" Leo asked. "Even when we go home?"

"No, don't worry, it's just part of the magic whilst you are here with us," Emerald said soothingly. "And best of all, time stops in your world whilst you are here, so you have time to do all the crafting you please and nobody will worry about you."

"Time to do as much crafting as we like!" Alice's eyes were shining. "But how did you know who we are?"

"Oh, that's thanks to the Glitterbugs!" said Emerald with a wink.

Leo frowned. "The Glitter . . . who?"

Emerald chuckled. "Follow me! I'll introduce you."

The little creature skipped over to a doorway into the enormous glittery hive. Alice and Leo shared a glance. Then they followed, tingling with excitement.

Inside, the hive seemed to glow with multicoloured light, as the sun shone

through the walls. *It's
like the whole building is a
stained-glass window!* thought Alice.

"Whoa!" cried Leo as he spotted
the Glitterbugs. "They're so cute!"
They were everywhere,
crawling across the
walls, snoozing on the
ground and flying
in circles high up
in the hive. They
looked like normal
bugs – ladybirds,
grasshoppers
and dragonflies

– but each was the size of a cat, with beautiful, shimmering bodies and sparkly wings.

"Hello!" said Alice, and the Glitterbugs waved their antennae in reply.

"They look just like the butterfly that took your sea glass," whispered Leo.

"Oh, you mean Hopscotch!" said Emerald. "Here he is now . . ."

As if on cue, a Glitterbug came swooping down to land. It was Hopscotch the butterfly. He put Alice's sea glass down carefully on the ground. Here in Cobbletown, it was the size of a small boulder.

Hopscotch lowered his antennae, looking bashful. He shuffled his legs around and gave a series of high-pitched trills and squeaks.

"Hopscotch says he's sorry," said Emerald. "He only took your sea glass so that you would come and visit us here in Cobbletown. He thought you'd like it here. But he wants to give you back your treasure now."

"Thank you, Hopscotch," said Alice.

"We forgive you," said Leo. "This place is incredible!" He stroked the butterfly's wings. They were as soft as velvet.

Hopscotch quivered and chirped, and a cloud of tiny pink hearts floated up from his antennae, like bubbles.

"That means he's happy!" said Emerald. "The Glitterbugs just love your craft shed, you know. They like to peek in through the window when they're out and about in Crystal Bay!"

"What's that one doing?" asked Leo.

He was watching a sparkling green caterpillar as it tucked a golden medal into a honeycomb-shaped pocket on the wall of the hive. Now that Leo looked around, he saw lots more pockets just like it.

"Allow me to explain," said Emerald proudly. "The Glitterbugs collect things from Crystal Bay. Forgotten things and thrown-away things. Bits and bobs and odds and ends. Each Glitterbug collects in a different part of town. And while they collect, they look out for any humans who have problems. That's where we come in!"

Emerald puffed out her chest.
"We're the Pixies, and
we love to help!
It's up to us to fix
the problems,
and we use our
magical crafting
tools to do it. We
take the objects that
the Glitterbugs bring

us, and we turn them into *new* things.
Magical things that will fix the problem!"

"Wow, you're *magical* crafters!" Alice's
eyes grew wide, as a thought came to
her. "So, if there was someone who was

having a hard time at school . . ."

"Someone who was finding it difficult to make friends . . ." added Leo.

To their surprise, Emerald seemed to droop. "Oh dear," she muttered. "*Is* there someone like that? I don't know how we've missed them!"

"Don't worry," said Leo, laying an arm around Emerald's little shoulders. "Ellie's only just moved to Crystal Bay. That must be why the Glitterbugs haven't spotted her yet."

That seemed to cheer the Pixie up. "All right then. We can definitely help with that!" She nodded with determination.

"I know . . . I'll make a magical bracelet! One that will give her the confidence to make friends." She stopped, suddenly looking shy. "I don't suppose you two would like to help, would you?"

Alice and Leo didn't hesitate. "Of course!"

"Splendiferous!"

Emerald hopped up and down with excitement, her bracelets jingling. "No time to lose!" she said. "First we'll need some thread. It's over there, Alice. And could you fetch some beads, Leo?"

Emerald pointed to some honeycomb

pockets, and the friends ran over.

Alice began pulling out a strand of red thread, so thick it was like a rope, and Leo lifted out a green wooden bead as big as a football.

"I know . . ." Alice looked thoughtfully at Leo. "The sea glass helped us both to make a friend, didn't it?"

"A *best* friend," said Leo.

"So maybe it could do the same for Ellie?"

Leo grinned. He had been thinking the same thing as Alice. "Could we put it on the magical bracelet?"

"Chokers and chains!"

exclaimed Emerald. "I just knew there was something special about you two!" She rapped her knuckles on the beautiful blue glass. "Now we've got everything we need, I'll show you my workshop."

The friends carried the materials through the town square and down a cobbled side street. The cobbles were made out of beach shells glued to a wide strip of grey felt, Leo noticed.

Emerald stopped beside an old wooden jewellery box and lifted a big golden latch, propping up the lid so that they could all scramble inside.

"Wow!" said Leo as the friends followed Emerald into the workshop. It was warm and cosy inside, with a sofa and armchairs made from cardboard.

The pink silk lining of the jewellery box was decorated with delicate silver chains, which hung above them and twinkled with charms and gemstones in every colour.

Emerald was already bustling around a little jewellery-making table. She put the pliers down next to the hammer and adjusted the lens of her golden magnifying glass. "Now then," she said, her green eyes sparkling. "Let's get crafting!"

But just as Leo was about to slide the first colourful wooden bead on to the end of the thread, Alice froze. "Can you hear that?" she said.

Everyone listened. At first there was just a distant, quiet thumping noise. But each thump grew louder and louder, as though some huge creatures were stomping down the street. Soon the whole jewellery box was trembling with each sound.

"Oh, bother my bangles!" whimpered Emerald. "This is terrible!" She looked suddenly frightened, her pointed ears lying flat against her head.

"What's the—" began Leo. But before he could finish, the whole jewellery box

rose into the air. Alice, Leo and Emerald
fell, rolling head over heels and out
through the open door.

They landed on their bottoms on the
seashell cobbles.

As they scrambled to their feet, a cold
shadow fell over them.

"Well, well," said a deep, booming
voice. "What have we here?"

Chapter Four
Grimble and Grumble

Bending over the friends were two huge, scowling creatures, each holding one end of the jewellery box. The smaller creature was twice the size of Emerald, and the larger was even bigger, as tall as Alice and Leo put together.

"Who are *they*?" asked Alice.

"Who are *we*?" growled the bigger creature. "You mean you don't know?"

"They're Nixies," whispered Emerald, huddled up in a ball and trembling with fear. "The *opposite* of Pixies. That's Grimble. And the other one's Grumble."

Grimble was tall and lanky. Grumble was short and broad. They each had a long nose and pointy ears, just like the Pixies.

But their thick purple hair was wild and clotted with bits of rubbish, stones and broken glass. Their clothes were ragged, grey and filthy. And their faces were twisted into the grumpiest frowns the friends had ever seen.

The Nixies tossed the jewellery box aside with a grunt.

"Hey!" shouted Leo. "Careful, you might break it!"

Grimble shrieked with laughter. "Ooh, I do hope so!" she cackled.

"We LOVE breaking things!" roared Grumble, puffing out his chest. "And we're the best at it, too!"

Grimble stuck her nose up in the air and sniffed. "We could smell you Pixies were happy about something. All the way from our lovely rubbish dump!"

"You're not making something, are you?" said Grumble, jabbing a big hairy finger at Emerald and making the little Pixie flinch away. "Something we can break?"

Alice swallowed, plucking up as much courage as she could. "Why on earth would you want to break things that other people have made? Things they've put love and care into?"

"Because breaking stuff is brilliant!"

crowed Grimble.

"Smashing pots!" yelled Grumble.

"Smearing paintings!" called Grimble.

"Stomping sandcastles!"

"Squishing birthday cakes!"

"And best of all . . ." added Grumble,
"squelching hopes and dreams and
friendship!"

"Eurgh, friendship!" cried Grimble.
"Yuck, hopes and dreams!" She
screwed up her face and shook her
messy purple hair.

"These silly old Pixies keep
fixing things so they can be
loved again," Grumble

complained. "So we have to smash them up all over again!"

"Go back to your rubbish dump, Nixies!" shouted Leo. "We're trying to help someone!"

Grimble blew a raspberry.

PTHHHHT!

"Helping is the worst. Come on, Grumble, let's break something!"

The two huge creatures reached behind them. Each pulled out a big hammer with a long wooden handle and a huge stone head. Dark magical sparks flared around the hammer heads, like flies buzzing around rotten food.

Emerald was still curled up, shivering with fear. Alice and Leo looked at each other.

"How can we stop them?" asked Alice.

Then they heard a familiar burst of squeaks from behind them. Looking back, they saw Hopscotch fluttering up the road.

Leo felt his heart sink. "Uh oh . . . I think Hopscotch is coming to help!"

"Go back!" Alice shouted, waving her arms at the butterfly. "It's too dangerous!"

But it was too late. The Nixies had spotted the Glitterbug, and a pair of slow, sly smiles spread across their hairy faces.

"Perfect!" snarled Grimble. "Get him, Grumble."

Grumble thrust out his hammer like a magic wand, and . . .

ZZZZAPP!

A bolt of magic struck Hopscotch with an explosion of black sparks.

"Got him!" crowed Grumble.

"No!" cried Leo.

The butterfly jerked and shuddered in

the air. His bright colours were fading, like a sky clouding over, and in a moment he had turned entirely grey. His antennae trembled, and a burst of tiny black storm clouds came streaming out.

"What have you done to him?" Alice demanded. She reached out to Hopscotch, but to her surprise the little creature darted away, squeaking crossly.

"Oh, nothing much," said Grimble, with a nasty grin.

"Just broken his friendship with the Pixies," said Grumble. "Smashed it to smithereens!"

"But that's horrible!" said Leo.

"Thank you," said Grumble proudly. "And now let's cause some more trouble!"

"Hopscotch," shouted Grimble. "Fetch!" The big hairy Nixie pointed to some objects that lay glinting on the ground.

"My magical tools!" squealed Emerald.

But it was too late. Before Alice or Leo could get to them, Hopscotch dived and scooped them all up in his little legs – the pliers, the hammer and the magnifying glass.

"Oh, please give them back!" yelped Emerald. "You can't break them anyway! They're too magical to be broken."

"We know that, silly," growled Grumble.

"We can't smash them," sneered Grimble. "But we can still get rid of them."

"Fly away, little

Gloomybug!" sang Grumble. "Hide those tools in Crystal Bay, where no one will find them, come what may!"

"Now Emerald can't make or mend like she could," chanted Grimble. "So the jewellery we smash will stay smashed up for good!"

"Look out!" yelled Alice.

Hopscotch came swooping low, making the friends duck. Their hair ruffled in the wind as he passed overhead. When they looked back, they saw him flying off around the corner, still clutching on tight to Emerald's tools.

"Off he goes to Crystal Bay," called

Grumble. "You'll never get those tools back now!"

A swirling wind began to blow around Grimble and Grumble, as they snorted and cackled with glee. Their feet slowly lifted off the ground, then –

WHOOOOOOSH!

– they vanished.

There was a long silence. Emerald hung her head, and the friends looked at each other in shock.

"Poor Hopscotch," said Leo at last.

"And poor Ellie," said Alice. "Without those tools, Emerald can't make the magical bracelet to help her."

"Oh, this is awful!" wailed Emerald, hugging her knees. "What am I going to do?"

Alice put her arm around the little Pixie's shoulders. "Don't worry," she said gently. "We'll save Hopscotch."

"And we'll get your tools back too," added Leo. "We promise."

Chapter Five
The Gloomybug Trail

"Do you really mean it?" said a voice from behind Alice and Leo.

The friends turned to see that a crowd of Pixies had gathered behind them, all looking terribly worried.

"Of course we do," said Alice fiercely. "We won't let Grimble and Grumble get away with this!"

"You fix problems for people in Crystal Bay," said Leo, "so let us fix this problem for you."

Emerald wiped a tear from her eye. "Toe rings and bobby pins! I'm so glad you two came here. Thank you, thank you!"

"No problem," said Alice, standing up. "But where do you think Hopscotch has gone?"

Emerald frowned in thought. "Well, he might be a Gloomybug, but he's still Hopscotch. And Hopscotch collects things from Crystal Bay Primary School.

Maybe that's where he's gone?"

"It's worth a try," said Leo.

"I'll come with you," said Emerald, scrambling to her feet. "Maybe I can help out with some Pixie Magic."

"Brilliant," said Alice. "But how do we get back to Crystal Bay?"

Emerald smiled for the first time since Grimble and Grumble had arrived. "Follow me . . ."

The other Pixies waved and cheered as the three of them set off along the road.

"Good luck!"

"Bring Hopscotch back safely!"

"Thank you, Alice and Leo!"

"We'll do our best!" Leo called back.

Emerald led them down a narrow, winding alleyway, until they came back out on to the quayside. They hopped down on to the sandy beach. And there, painted on the wall, was a mural just like the one they had come through when they arrived in Cobbletown.

"It's Crystal Bay!" grinned Alice. "Wow . . . I can even smell the sea air!"

"Come on, you two," said Emerald, taking their hands. "You worked out how to get here. It's the same to get back. We just touch the spot on the mural where we want to go. Ready?"

"Ready!" said the friends. Then they each put a hand on the painting, right where the little picture of the school was painted . . .

WHOOOOOOSH!

In a blur of twinkling lights, Alice and Leo came stumbling to a halt. Looking around, they saw that they were in the empty playground at school.

"I love magic!" said Alice. "And I don't feel so dizzy this time."

"I guess we're getting used to it," said Leo. "Hey, where did Emerald go?"

"Down here!" came a little voice.

The friends peered at the ground. Emerald was tiny now – shorter than a pencil. Leo bent to scoop her up, and she sat cross-legged in the palm of his hand.

"Do you see Hopscotch?" she asked.

"No," said Leo. "But what's that?"

They all stared hard at something hovering beside a side door. It was a little trail of grey specks, like ash floating in the air.

"That must be Hopscotch's trail!"

said Alice suddenly. "It was all golden before, but now he's a Gloomybug, I suppose it's turned grey like the rest of him."

"Good thinking!" cried Emerald. "Let's follow it."

The friends edged along the wall. The door was ajar, and they crept into a brightly lit corridor. Hopscotch's trail floated like a stream of dust, in through a classroom door. Alice and Leo followed it inside.

It was their old reception classroom, with red beanbags on the floor, handprint tree paintings dangling from strings and cut-out letters of the alphabet attached to the window.

"It's strange being here after school," whispered Alice.

"Yes, it's never this quiet during the day," Leo agreed.

"Over there!" cried Emerald, pointing at an art cupboard on the far wall. The grey trail seemed to disappear through the open door.

"Got him!" said Leo, grinning. "Wait, do you hear that?"

Footsteps!

Someone was coming along the corridor outside. They could hear voices too, chatting away.

"That's Mrs Baker and Mr Sandhu!" hissed Alice. "They haven't gone home yet! If they see us, they'll want to know what we're doing here!"

"Where do we hide?" asked Leo, looking around desperately.

"Leave it to me!" said Emerald. "Just pop me on that desk, Leo."

As Leo gently lowered the Pixie, Emerald was busy untying a little green velvet bag from her tool belt. Reaching inside, she pulled out a fistful of golden dust.

"Just a little magic I

keep for emergencies!" said Emerald.

"Now, hold on to your hats!" She held

the dust to her mouth and puffed,

blowing it at Alice and Leo.

WHOOOOOOSH!

Golden sparkles swirled through the

air, and the friends felt their stomachs

leap into their mouths. They were falling

and falling, and the world was getting

bigger and bigger . . .

No, that's not it, Alice realised. *We're*

shrinking!

Chapter Six
Trapped!

As the magic faded, Alice and Leo blinked and rubbed at their eyes. They looked around.

Emerald came sliding down one leg of the desk, hugging it like a fireman's pole. *Thump!* Her little boots landed on the carpet, right next to them.

"It's like we're back in Cobbletown!" said Leo.

Sure enough, Emerald was only a little shorter than the friends now, just as she had been when they first met her. But everything else looked huge! The chair legs were like tree trunks. The rough strands of the carpet rose up over the friends' ankles, like long grass.

"We're smaller than kittens," said Alice in wonder.

There was a click and a squeal of hinges as the classroom door opened . . .

"Take cover!" hissed Leo.

All three of them hid behind the desk leg, peering cautiously out.

Mrs Baker and Mr Sandhu came in, their footsteps clumping heavily. The teachers were gigantic now, so tall the friends could hardly see their faces.

They turned their backs to unclip paintings from the strings attached to the ceiling and replace them with leaf rubbing artwork.

"I am worried about Ellie, you know," Mrs Baker sighed, her voice a lot softer than it usually was.

"The new girl in your class?" Mr Sandhu asked.

"That's *our* Ellie," Alice whispered.

"Yes, she seems to be struggling to make friends," Mrs Baker said. "I do hope the other children are being friendly to her. Perhaps I'll speak to Ellie's dad."

"Good idea," Mr Sandhu replied warmly.

Leo's eyes were wide. "Do you think Mr Sandhu worries about *us* like that?" he breathed.

"Come on, you two, we have to hide," Emerald hissed, tugging anxiously at her ears.

"We've got to get to the art cupboard," said Alice.

"When I say go . . ." said Leo. "Go!"

The three of them dashed across the carpet and slipped through the open door of the cupboard.

It was dark inside, but as their eyes adjusted, they found themselves surrounded by a forest of objects towering over them – giant paintbrushes propped up in a jam jar, a stack of massive crayons, fluffy pipe cleaners and enormous glue sticks.

"This is where the grey trail went," whispered Alice. "So Hopscotch must be here somewhere. Let's split up and look for him."

Leo clambered over a stack of soft white erasers, each as big as a hay bale, while Emerald sifted through a box of sequins the size of dinner plates. Alice peered at some grey dust stuck to a box of paper clips. Hopscotch's trail!

"Where is he . . . ?" wondered Leo.

Then Alice let out a yelp of excitement. "Look!"

She pointed to a heap of cotton balls in a box. Perched right on top of them was a gleaming pair of golden pliers.

"And here!" Leo held up a shining magnifying glass that had been hidden in the thicket of pipe cleaners.

"My magical tools!" squeaked Emerald. She scrambled up the cotton ball hill, took the pliers and tucked them away in her tool belt.

"Nice one!" said Leo, giving Alice a high five. "Now we've only got the hammer left to find. I wonder where it is?"

Then a shadow fell across them. Looking up, the friends saw a familiar creature flapping in mid-air, holding a little golden hammer tightly with his front legs . . .

"Hopscotch!" shouted Alice and Leo at the same time.

Before they could catch hold of the Gloomybug, Hopscotch darted out of the cupboard, tiny lightning bolts streaking from his antennae. He swung the hammer – **THWACK!** – straight into the cupboard door, and – **WHUMPH!** – the door slammed shut.

Everything went dark. Then came a soft *clunk* from outside.

"That's the latch," cried Alice. "He's trapped us in here!"

Emerald whimpered with fear.

"Hold on, Emerald," said Leo. "I'm coming for you." Clambering up the cotton wool balls in darkness, Leo cast about until his hand closed on Emerald's. Together, they picked their way back down to the floor of the cupboard.

"Pendants and pocket watches!" gasped Emerald. "I didn't like that one bit! But I feel better now I'm with you two."

"Looks like we're stuck here," said Leo, frowning. "Unless . . . Could you make us big again, Emerald?"

"The cupboard's too small for that," said Alice, shaking her head. "And the teachers are still outside!" They could hear Mr Sandhu humming to himself. "If only it wasn't so dark . . ."

"There is *some* light," said Leo. "There, at the edge of the door."

A thin line of brightness was just visible.

"Hey," said Alice. Her heart quickened. "This cupboard has a handle on the inside as well. That's good!" She pointed up at the silver handle, gleaming a little in the line of daylight.

"But we can't reach the handle," Leo pointed out.

From where they were standing on the floor, it was high over their heads. And if they climbed up the shelves at the back of the cupboard, it would be too far to jump to the handle.

"Not without help," Alice agreed, her eyes darting about the cupboard.

Leo clapped. "Alice is going to invent something!"

"Oh, how clever," Emerald squealed. "What can we do to help?"

Alice looked around, her mind whirring. She spotted the pipe cleaners again, and her eyes grew wide. "Follow me!"

The friends darted over to the pipe cleaners and lifted one from the pile. It was about the length of a broom handle to them. Alice got to work at one end, bending it over to make a hook.

"Now, Leo, if you get on my shoulders and then Emerald, you sit on Leo's shoulders and hold the pipe cleaner, you should be able to reach the handle and pull it down," said Alice.

"Like a circus act!" Leo cried. "Brilliant!"

Using a stack of notebooks at the back of the cupboard, they carefully climbed and balanced until Leo was on Alice's

shoulders and Emerald was perched atop Leo's shoulders, holding the hooked pipe cleaner.

Alice began to walk slowly towards the door.

"Balance, everyone, balance!" Leo said as they started to sway a little.

They made it to the door. Emerald reached up, up and with a squeak of celebration, she hooked the pipe cleaner over the handle and pulled down. The door swung open with a creak, and light flooded in.

"Yes!" cried Alice as Emerald and Leo jumped down.

But her excitement died as she saw Mrs Baker turn. "What on earth was that noise?"

"My word!" said Mr Sandhu. "That cupboard seems to have opened itself!"

And then the friends' hearts stopped as they saw him striding across the floor, heading straight towards them . . .

Chapter Seven
A Sticky Situation

"Run!" whispered Leo.

He grabbed Emerald's little hand with his own. Alice heaved at the heap of cotton wool balls, sending them spilling across the floor.

"Mice!" gasped Mr Sandhu.

"Where?" cried Mrs Baker.

While Mr Sandhu pointed at the cotton wool ball explosion, the three friends slipped out of the cupboard. They darted across the carpet, past the desks and the chairs and through the doorway.

Outside, they skidded to a halt and pressed up against the wall, panting.

"Phew!" breathed Alice. "I don't think they spotted us. And look – there's Hopscotch's trail again!"

They could all see it floating in the air, a stream of grey dust that drifted around the corner.

"Let's stay small," said Leo. "In case

any other teachers show up!"

They set off, following the trail.

"Ooh, I do hope we can get my hammer back," muttered Emerald as they turned a corner.

"We can do it," said Leo. "And we'll save Hopscotch, too. We've got to turn that Gloomybug back into a Glitterbug!"

"There he goes!" shouted Alice.

Up ahead, Hopscotch streaked into another corridor, still holding the golden hammer.

"He won't get away this time," said Alice. "Follow me!"

They raced into the narrow corridor. There was only one room leading off it. *Miss Theobald*, said the little golden sign on the half-open door. They saw the last wisps of Hopscotch's trail settling around the doorframe. Light spilled from inside.

Leo frowned. "The head teacher's office!" he whispered. "And I think Miss Theobald is in there!"

Sure enough, they could hear their head teacher's voice chatting away inside the office.

"We can't go in, can we?" asked Alice.

"I think we have to," said Leo. "Or we'll

never get Hopscotch back."

"We could be really quiet," said Emerald eagerly.

Alice looked at Emerald, her ears pricked with hope. She swallowed her doubts.

"All right," she said bravely. "For Hopscotch . . . Let's do it!"

Holding their breath, the friends tiptoed through the half-open door into the head teacher's office. There was a wastepaper basket beside them, and they ducked down behind it.

Leo's heart was

racing. *What if we get caught in here?* he worried. *But we've got to be brave for Hopscotch!*

Miss Theobald was leaning back in her chair, talking on her phone. She hung up, put the phone down and turned to her laptop. Her glasses reflected the white glow of the screen as she put a set of headphones on and began to tap at the keyboard.

"Where's Hopscotch?" Leo whispered.

The friends looked all around – from the lamp on Miss Theobald's desk, to the comfy blue chairs opposite, to the shelves on the wall loaded with neatly labelled files, books, trophies and . . .

"There!" hissed Alice.

She pointed to the big golden Sports Day cup. Poking up from inside it were two quivering little antennae.

"Quick," said Leo, "before he flies off!"

They dashed behind Miss Theobald's desk, where she couldn't see them.

"No!" squeaked Emerald.

The friends' hearts sank as they saw Hopscotch crawl out of the cup and take off, wings fluttering as he came down to land on top of the desk. He was still clutching the golden hammer. The Gloomybug's head appeared over the edge of the desk, and his long curly tongue came rolling out.

"Don't stick your tongue out at us!" Alice scolded.

Leo frowned with worry. "Miss Theobald's going to see him! We've got to get up there."

The head teacher's umbrella was propped against the side of the desk. The friends and Emerald helped each other to scramble up its folds until they reached the top of the desk, where they hid behind a mug full of pens.

Miss Theobald was completely absorbed by her laptop while Hopscotch crawled around her desk. He dragged the hammer after him as he sniffed at paper clips and nudged a rubber band with his front legs.

"She's going to spot him!" hissed Alice.

Emerald looked anxious now. "Oh, pinky rings!" she said. "You don't think . . . She wouldn't *swat* him, would she?"

"Oh no!" cried Leo, pointing.

The others gasped.

Hopscotch was crawling through a tape dispenser. But halfway through, his fluttering wings got stuck on the strip of tape stretched above him. He dropped the hammer in surprise. As he wriggled, his wings got more stuck than ever.

Alice winced as she saw Miss Theobald sitting back, leaning over to rummage in her handbag.

"Quick!" squealed Emerald. "Before—"

But it was too late. Hopscotch let out a little trill of panicked squeaks.

Miss Theobald froze. Slowly she took off her headphones. "What on earth . . ." she muttered.

"We've got to distract her," whispered Leo. "Here, give me your magnifying glass!"

Emerald pulled the magical object from her tool belt and handed it over.

Reaching around the side of the pen mug, Leo used the lens to focus light from the desk lamp. It made a little spot that danced across the surface. *Just like a spotlight on stage!* he thought. With a flick of his wrist, he moved the light spot right on to Miss Theobald's keyboard.

Miss Theobald blinked at the little spot of light.

Then she took off her glasses to rub her eyes. "Goodness, now I'm seeing things too," she murmured to herself. "Time for a tea break, I think."

Pushing her chair back, Miss Theobald got up and left the room.

"Nice work," said Alice. "Come on!"

They ran across the desk to the tape dispenser. Hopscotch was still batting his wings wildly, getting more and more tangled in the sticky tape.

"Be still, Hopscotch," said Leo, gently stroking the Gloomybug's velvety grey wing. "We'll save you."

Hopscotch stopped moving as Leo

spoke softly to him. Meanwhile, Emerald and Alice got to work peeling the sticky tape away from his body.

"I don't know how much time we have . . ." muttered Leo.

Alice's heart was thundering. *Any minute now, Miss Theobald might come back!* If she walked in now, she would spot them for sure.

"There!" cried Emerald. At last, they pulled the final bit of tape free from the Gloomybug. He opened and closed his wings slowly, his antennae twitching.

It felt good to see Hopscotch free. But all the same, Alice felt downcast.

Nothing's really changed, she thought.

"I wish we could make you understand," she said to Hopscotch. "The Pixies are your friends! You don't have to be a Gloomybug."

Hopscotch just cocked his head and looked at her with his big grey eyes.

Then, all at once, there was a tinkling noise like wind chimes and multicoloured sparkles fizzed in the air around Hopscotch. Colour flooded his wings, the patterns of pink and gold and blue chasing the grey away.

The friends' hearts leapt. Hopscotch was a Glitterbug again!

A single red heart rose up from Hopscotch's antennae, and he chirped happily. The friends and Emerald flung themselves at him and held his small, velvety body tightly.

"Oh, Hopscotch!" cried Emerald, burying her face in his soft wings.

But Alice was feeling anxious. "We'd better get out of here!"

Leo pointed at a little window above the desk, propped open with a stack of books. "Hopscotch can fly through there. What about the rest of us?"

Alice looked around the desk, her inventing brain buzzing into action.

"I know!" she said. "Give me a hand with this."

Together, she and Leo dragged a plastic ruler along the desk and balanced it on top of a pencil sharpener. Then, straining hard, they heaved a glass paperweight on to one end of the ruler to hold it down.

Hopscotch fluttered on to the desk lamp and watched from above.

"Brooches and bracelets, I can hear Miss Theobald!" cried Emerald. "She's coming back!"

Chapter Eight
Friendship Magic

Miss Theobald's footsteps came down the corridor, closer and closer . . .

"Follow my lead," said Alice. She climbed up on to the mug of pens and took a deep breath. Then she jumped as high as she could, landing hard on the end of the ruler.

TWWAAANG!

The plastic ruler bent

and sprang back,

throwing Alice

through the air. She

flailed her arms,

heart racing, then . . .

THUMP!

She landed on the

windowsill.

"Brilliant!" whooped Leo. He went

next, catapulting himself and dropping

neatly in a crouch beside Alice. Last

came Emerald. The little Pixie's eyes

were wide with fear – and excitement –

as she fell in a heap beside them.

"Chokers and chains,"

she gasped.

The office door opened, and Miss Theobald came in, holding a steaming mug of tea.

"No time to lose," whispered Alice. Leaning out of the window, she saw ivy climbing up the wall beside the frame. She edged out, took hold of the ivy and lowered herself down, wrapping her knees around the stalk as though it was a thick rope.

Leo helped Emerald on to the ivy, then followed himself, clambering down until

his feet felt the loose soil below the
windowsill.

"Phew!" said Alice, dusting herself off.
"We made it. But where's Hopscotch?"

As if in answer, the little Glitterbug
came soaring from the window, looped
the loop and dived down to land beside
them. This time, he left a sparkling
trail of glitter instead of grey dust.

"He really is himself
again!" laughed Leo,
nuzzling Hopscotch's
soft little head.

"But I don't
understand," said Alice.

"How did we break the spell? Why *isn't* Hopscotch a Gloomybug any more?"

Emerald smiled. "I know why! That sound and those sparkles can only come from one thing: the magic of kindness. It's because we freed him from that sticky tape! We did something kind for him, and that reminded him who his friends are. Now his friendship with the Pixies is mended!"

"Wow, I didn't know being kind could be magical!" Leo exclaimed.

"Well, that special kindness magic can only be created by people who know how to be the very best of friends," said

Emerald. "I *knew* you two were special!"

Hopscotch squeaked, and a whole cloud of red hearts rose from his antennae.

Alice and Leo grinned. They knew just how he felt!

". . . And the finishing touch," said Emerald a little later, sticking her tongue out in concentration. "The sea glass!"

After saving Hopscotch, the friends had travelled back through the mural to Cobbletown, along with Emerald and Hopscotch, of course. Now they were in the Pixie's jewellery box workshop. They watched, holding their breath, as Emerald carefully tied the sea glass into place.

Sparks of magic sizzled around Ellie's new bracelet, a rainbow of wooden beads on thread, with the sea glass dangling from it like a charm. Emerald pulled the thread tight with her pliers. "All done!" She laid down her pliers and wrapped up Alice and Leo in a big hug. "Thanks to you two!"

"We're just glad we could help," said Leo bashfully.

"It was nothing,"

added Alice.

"Dazzling diamonds!" cried Emerald. "You must be joking! Without you, I would have lost my magical tools for ever. Not to mention poor Hopscotch!"

The three of them lifted the bracelet between them and carried it carefully out into the street. A hushed crowd of Pixies and Glitterbugs was waiting for them, all staring with wide eyes. But when they saw the bracelet, a chorus of cheers and happy squeaks rose up, and they all started fluttering and scuttling and prancing in the street.

"Hurrah for Alice and Leo!"

"You did it!"

"Three cheers for the heroes of Cobbletown!"

"Thank you!" called Alice, waving. "We couldn't have done it without Emerald!" But her smile froze as she felt the wind pick up, tugging at her clothes and tangling her hair.

"Looks like Grimble and Grumble are back," said Leo as a whirlwind of old rubbish came roaring up the street, forcing the Pixies and Glitterbugs to back away.

The wind died suddenly, and the rubbish settled

to reveal Grimble and Grumble scowling ferociously.

"What have you meddlers *done*?" howled Grimble, tearing at her tufty purple hair.

"You're not supposed to be able to *make* things!" growled Grumble, pointing a thick hairy finger at the magical bracelet.

Leo stepped forward, clenching his fists. "We found Emerald's magical tools for her," he said.

"And we broke your horrible spell on Hopscotch," said Alice bravely, stepping up next to him. "You mean old Nixies can't destroy true friendship!"

Hopscotch fluttered out of the crowd to join them, twittering nervously. He nestled in between the friends, folding his colourful wings.

"Noooo!" roared Grimble.

"Now I *really* want to smash something!" shouted Grumble.

"We'll be back, you pests!" Grimble shook her huge fist and scowled all around at the Pixies and Glitterbugs, making them flinch. "You see if we're not!"

The rubbish began to whirl around them again,

faster and faster, until, with a flash like a lightning bolt, they had vanished into thin air.

"Good riddance," said Leo.

The friends turned to see the Pixies looking frightened, shuffling their feet and casting nervous glances all around.

"Don't worry," said Alice. "We won't let those meanies destroy Cobbletown."

"No way," agreed Leo. "We're your friends now. And we'll stick with you through thick and thin!"

Slowly, one by one, the Pixies began to smile.

"Do you mean it?" said one.

"Really and truly?" said another.

Emerald's big eyes were brimming with happy tears. "Oh, cufflinks!" she squeaked. "You two really are splendiferous!"

"Goodbye, Emerald," said Alice, and she gave the little Pixie one last hug. "Goodbye, Hopscotch." She stroked the Glitterbug's soft, furry back, and Hopscotch gave a happy squeak.

"We'd better take the bracelet back home now, to Crystal Bay," said Leo. "It's time for our tea."

"But we won't ever forget you and the

Pixies," said Alice.

"I know you won't," said Emerald, her green eyes twinkling. "In fact . . . I have a feeling you'll be back here in no time at all! You two understand kindness and crafting so well, you're almost like human Pixies!"

The next morning, Alice and Leo stood in the playground at Crystal Bay Primary School, looking all around for Ellie. The bell hadn't rung yet. Children ran and played, while parents chatted in little groups.

"The school seems smaller now, doesn't it?" said Leo, in a low voice. "It's weird being normal-sized!"

Alice nodded. Her fingers closed around the new bracelet in her coat pocket. "There she is!" she cried.

Ellie and her mum came in through the school gates, holding hands. Leo felt a rush of sadness as he saw that Ellie looked even more nervous than yesterday, clutching tight to her book bag and huddling close to her mum.

The friends ran over to her.

"Hello there," said Leo with a cheerful grin. "I'm Leo, and this is Alice. We heard you're new at school."

Ellie clung tighter to her mum and nodded shyly.

"We made you something," said Alice. "A welcome gift!" She held out the bracelet.

"How kind of you!" said Ellie's mum. She had curly red hair and freckles, just like Ellie.

Ellie hesitated. Then a smile spread across her face. She let go of her mum's hand and stepped forward to take the bracelet. "Thank you," she said quietly.

"Here." Alice helped her put it on, bending down to whisper in Ellie's ear.

"It's magic,
if you can
believe it!"
She gave
Ellie a wink.
 The
bell rang.
Alice and
Leo waved
goodbye to Ellie
and ran off to line up
for class.

 Leo looked back over his shoulder. He
saw Ellie standing by herself, looking
uncertain.

Then a football rolled past. Ellie stared at it. And slowly, her smile grew into a grin. She stepped over and kicked the football back to a girl who was chasing after it.

The last thing the friends saw, before they went into class, was Ellie going over to the girl with the football and giving her a wave. *She's saying hello!* thought Alice, her heart bursting with happiness. Then Ellie and the girl began to walk into class together, beaming and chattering as they went.

"The Pixie Magic worked!" said Leo, and he and Alice grinned at each other.

They had helped Ellie make her first friend at Crystal Bay Primary School. And their own friendship was stronger than ever – even without their special piece of sea glass.

"Do you think we really will go back to Cobbletown soon?" wondered Leo.

"I'm sure of it," said Alice. "And I don't know about you . . . but I can't wait!"

THE END

Make Your Own Friendship Bracelet!

Emerald, Alice and Leo made a magical bracelet to help a new girl feel welcome at school. Make your very own magic friendship bracelet* in five simple steps. You could give it to your best friend!

You will need:

- **Colourful paper** (e.g. old magazines, wrapping paper or wallpaper)
- **Pencil**
- **Scissors**
- **A glue stick**
- **String**

Adult supervision is recommended when glue, scissors and other sharp points are in use.

1. Ask a grown-up to help you cut your paper into long triangles. The wider the triangle, the bigger the bead will be.
2. Take one triangle and lay the pencil along the short edge. Roll the paper around the pencil twice.
3. Cover the unrolled part of the triangle with glue, then tightly roll the paper strip around the pencil. Add a bit more glue to the point so the bead doesn't unravel.
4. Slide the bead off the pencil and let it dry. Make a few more beads while you wait.
5. Thread the beads on to string to make a beautiful bracelet!

Look out for the next Pixie Magic book:
Dotty and the Sweet Surprise

Can Alice, Leo and Dotty the
Pottery Pixie work together to
make the Crystal Bay winter fair
extra special?